TWELVE
CHAMBER DUETS

RECENT RESEARCHES IN THE MUSIC OF THE BAROQUE ERA

Robert L. Marshall, general editor

A-R Editions, Inc., publishes six quarterly series—

Recent Researches in the Music of the Middle Ages and Early Renaissance
Margaret Bent, general editor

Recent Researches in the Music of the Renaissance
James Haar, general editor

Recent Researches in the Music of the Baroque Era
Robert L. Marshall, general editor

Recent Researches in the Music of the Classical Era
Eugene K. Wolf, general editor

Recent Researches in the Music of the Nineteenth and Early Twentieth Centuries
Rufus Hallmark, general editor

Recent Researches in American Music
H. Wiley Hitchcock, general editor—

which make public music that is being brought to light
in the course of current musicological research.

Each volume in the *Recent Researches* is devoted
to works by a single composer or to a single genre of composition,
chosen because of its potential interest to scholars and performers,
and prepared for publication according to the standards that govern
the making of all reliable historical editions.

Subscribers to this series, as well as patrons of subscribing institutions,
are invited to apply for information about the "Copyright-Sharing Policy"
of A-R Editions, Inc., under which the contents of this volume
may be reproduced free of charge for study or performance.

Correspondence should be addressed:

A-R EDITIONS, INC.
315 West Gorham Street
Madison, Wisconsin 53703

RECENT RESEARCHES IN THE MUSIC OF THE BAROQUE ERA • VOLUME LIII

Agostino Steffani

TWELVE CHAMBER DUETS

Edited by Colin Timms

A-R EDITIONS, INC. • MADISON

Library of Congress Cataloging-in-Publication Data

Steffani, Agostino, 1654–1728.
    [Duets, voices, continuo. Selections]
    Twelve chamber duets.

    (Recent researches in the music of the Baroque Era,
ISSN 0484–0828 ; v. 53)
    For 2 sopranos (1st–4th and 7th–8th works), soprano
and tenor (5th–6th and 9th–10th), soprano and alto (11th),
or alto and bass (12th) and continuo.
    Edited from mss. in the British Library, London:
1st–6th works from holograph (RM 23.k.14), 7th–12th
from copyist's ms. (RM 23.k.7).
    Unfigured bass realized for harpsichord (also bass
stringed instrument recommended by the editor).
    Words also printed as texts with English transla-
tions, p.
    Bibliography: p.
    Contents: Pria ch'io faccia altrui palese—Quanto
care al cor voi siete—Ribellatevi, o pensieri—Su,
ferisci, alato arciero—[etc.]
    1. Vocal duets with continuo.   I. Timms, Colin.
II. Series.
M2.R238   vol. 53   [M1529.2]   86–754081
ISBN 0–89579–215–X

Contents

Preface
    Agostino Steffani   vii
    The Chamber Duet   vii
    Steffani's Chamber Duets   viii
    Sources   x
    Editorial Methods   xi
    Notes on Performance   xii
    Critical Notes   xiii
    Acknowledgments   xiv
    Notes   xv
Texts and Translations   xvi
Plate Ia   xxii
Plate Ib   xxii
Plate IIa   xxiii
Plate IIb   xxiii

Pria ch'io faccia altrui palese	[Soprano, Soprano]	1
Quanto care al cor voi siete	[Soprano, Soprano]	10
Ribellatevi, o pensieri	[Soprano, Soprano]	20
Su, ferisci, alato arciero	[Soprano, Soprano]	26
E perché non m'uccidete	[Soprano, Tenor]	34
E così mi compatite?	[Soprano, Tenor]	43
Saldi marmi, che coprite	[Soprano, Soprano]	51
Ravvediti, mio core	[Soprano, Soprano]	67
Vorrei dire un non so che	[Soprano, Tenor]	79
Occhi belli, non più	[Soprano, Tenor]	89
Begl'occhi, oh Dio, non più	[Soprano, Alto]	103
Aure, voi che volate	[Alto, Bass]	115

Preface

Agostino Steffani

Steffani could be regarded as the Corelli of the voice: what Corelli did for the trio sonata, Steffani did for the vocal duet. Both contributed handsomely to the dissemination of the late seventeenth-century Italian style. Corelli's sonatas were printed (and reprinted) in northern Europe. Steffani worked there for most of his life; his duets were circulated in innumerable manuscripts, and his Hanover operas (which also display features of the French style) were a powerful stimulus to the development of opera throughout northern Germany. His duets and operas directly influenced a large number of composers, including Keiser, Telemann, Handel, and Bononcini, and make him a crucial figure in the history of music in the mid-to-late baroque period.

Born at Castelfranco, near Padua, in 1654 (the year after Corelli's birth), Steffani was taken at about the age of thirteen to Munich, where he had organ lessons with the kapellmeister, Johann Kaspar Kerll. In 1672 he was sent to Rome to study with Ercole Bernabei, *maestro di cappella* of St. Peter's, but two years later Bernabei himself was appointed kapellmeister at Munich, and Steffani returned there with him. He was made court organist soon after his arrival and director of chamber music in 1681. Among the works that he wrote during his Munich years (1667–88) are printed books of polychoral psalms and *concertato* motets, five operas, and some of his chamber duets.

At Munich Steffani also undertook the first of many diplomatic missions when he agreed to explore the possibility of a marriage between the Elector Maximilian II Emanuel and Princess Sophie Charlotte of Hanover. This venture came to nought. But by the time that Bernabei was succeeded as kapellmeister by his son in 1688, the way had been paved for Steffani to move to Hanover as director ("Kapellmeister") of Duke Ernst August's new Italian opera company. During the next nine years, the heyday of the Hanover opera, he probably composed seven three-act works and a couple of one-act entertainments,[1] and many more chamber duets.

At the same time Steffani also became increasingly involved in diplomatic activities, so much so that for Carnival in 1696 he was replaced as kapellmeister by Pietro Torri, his successor as organist at Munich and currently kapellmeister of the Bavarian court at Brussels. Steffani had by this time been appointed Hanoverian "envoy extraordinary" to the latter court, and as the storm-clouds of the War of the Spanish Succession gathered on the horizon, he became responsible for trying to persuade the Elector Maximilian to support the emperor rather than Louis XIV. Despite the most prodigious efforts, he failed.

Bitterly disappointed and utterly exhausted, he returned to Hanover in July 1702 and threw himself later that autumn into the revision and into the preparation of a new complete manuscript collection of his chamber duets.[2]

The rest of his life was devoted largely to the Church. A priest since 1680, he had been made Abbot of Lepsingen in 1683 and an apostolic protonotary by 1695. When he moved to Düsseldorf in the spring of 1703, he was appointed president of the Spiritual Council for the Palatinate and for the Duchies of Jülich and Berg, and less than four years later he was consecrated as Bishop of Spiga. In April 1709 he became apostolic vicar of northern Germany, with responsibility for all the Catholic communities in Prussia, the Palatinate, and the Brunswick lands. He moved back to Hanover in November of that year and, apart from a brief period in Italy (1722–25), was based there until his death in 1728.

Except for the opera *Tassilone* (performed at Düsseldorf in 1709)[3] and a slightly later chamber duet, he appears to have composed very little after moving to Düsseldorf until the last year or two of his life, when he was elected president of the Academy of Ancient Music in London.[4] In addition to sending the Academy copies of his earlier works, he wrote a few new ones including, probably, his famous *Stabat Mater*. Doubtless he would have continued to compose, but his health deteriorated during the winter of 1727–28, and on 12 February he died of apoplexy in Frankfurt-am-Main.

The Chamber Duet

The chamber duet, as David Burrows has pointed out, is not a distinct form but "a special case of the secular Italian cantata."[5] The cantata was one of the principal forms of the musical baroque. As a species of vocal chamber music it was a counterpart to the opera and oratorio and performed a function previously fulfilled by the Renaissance madrigal. Although the word "cantata" was used by Alessandro Grandi before 1620, it acquired a fixed meaning only after about 1650, when it came to denote "a setting of a monologue or dialogue text, sometimes with narrative, as a succession of recitatives and arias or aria-like sections, usually for one or two voices, more rarely for three or four, accompanied by continuo and occasionally by obbligato or orchestral instruments."[6]

It is partly because the chamber duet is not a distinct form that it would be difficult to give a comprehensive account of its history.[7] The term appears to have been used first by Maurizio Cazzati, in the title of his *Duetti per camera*, op. 66 (Bologna: Giacomo Monti, 1677), but since the beginning of the century duets had been published as "madrigali," "arie," "scherzi," and "canzonette"—

designations that indicate the forms and styles in which they were composed.

The emergence of the form of the later *seicento* solo cantata and its influence on that of the chamber duet are reflected in the printed sources by the first appearance, in 1651, of the word "duetti" in the title of a printed book (Barbara Strozzi's *Cantate, ariette e duetti,* op. 2), by the increasingly frequent use of the word "cantata" applied to duets, and by the gradual abandonment of the earlier designations. Strozzi's works are among the last examples of secular music to have been printed in Venice in the seventeenth century. For more than a decade manuscripts had been the normal means by which such music had been circulated, and, furthermore, Rome had been the principal center for the cultivation of vocal chamber music. The leading cantata composers of Rome—Luigi Rossi, Carissimi, Cesti, and Stradella—all wrote duets and set an example that was followed by Steffani and by composers elsewhere, especially at Bologna. Eleven books containing duets were published at Bologna between Cazzati's *Duetti* and Clari's celebrated *Duetti e terzetti da camera* of 1720. Most of these books also included music for other numbers of voices, and some were based on "moral" or "spiritual" texts.

The chamber duets of the later seventeenth and early eighteenth centuries can be divided into two rough groups according to their texts. If the text is a dialogue, the singers will have different words and may represent different characters; if the text is a monologue, both singers will have the same words in the duet movements and may represent one and the same character. It would seem that the former were more frequently called *"cantate a due"* and the latter *"duetti da camera,"* although in Bolognese sources these terms are sometimes reversed. While the *cantata a due* could resemble a dramatic scene, the *duetto da camera* was simply an expansion of the solo cantata, and its popularity was due partly to the fact that, like the trio sonata, it afforded a range of textural, formal, and harmonic possibilities that were denied to its solo counterpart.

The most important of these possibilities, perhaps, was that of vocal counterpoint. Throughout the history of the duet in the baroque period the voices frequently move in parallel thirds and sixths, engage in motivic interplay or repartee, and employ loosely constructed imitative textures of the *"a risposta"* variety—"whereby the two *concertante* violin parts [in a trio sonata] begin, not in imitation at the fifth, but by alternation at the unison, with each part presenting the material *solo* over the bass before turning to more consequential imitation and *fugato* (which latter then has the effect of *stretto*)."[8]

The development of more elaborate contrapuntal textures in the sphere of the duet occurred toward the end of the seventeenth century when, as Burney observed,

> a species of learned and elaborate *Chamber Duets* for voices began to be in favour. The first that I have found, of this kind, were composed by John [Giovanni] Bononcini, and published at Bologna in 1691. Soon after, those of the admirable Abate Steffani were dispersed in manuscript throughout Europe. These were followed by the duets of Clari, Handel, Marcello, Gasparini, Lotti, Hasse, and Durante.[9]

Bononcini's duets were probably not the first of this kind for, as we shall see, at least one of Steffani's duets appears to have been composed before 1688 and probably others were too. Compared with the music of Burney's day, Bononcini's duets must have appeared "learned and elaborate," but they now seem less consistently contrapuntal than those of Steffani and closer to the *cantata a due*. According to Schmitz, it was through Steffani's duets that the genre became associated with the notion of a display of contrapuntal skill, and the texture of his duets should for this reason be regarded as the hallmark of the form in its highest perfection.[10]

By the mid-eighteenth century the chamber duet, like the solo cantata, was virtually dead. Antonio Lotti and Benedetto Marcello published duets in 1705 and 1717, respectively, and Bononcini issued a second book, of solo cantatas as well as duets, in London in 1721. Many more composers left such works in manuscript, including Handel, who possessed a copy of Steffani duets and imitated them in his own duets of 1708–12.[11] His London duets of 1741–45 must be among the latest examples of the genre. The fact that some of the choruses in *Messiah* (1741) are based on duets by Handel himself is a clear indication that that style, at least, of late baroque music owed a very great deal to the influence of Steffani and his chamber duets.

Steffani's Chamber Duets

Steffani can be reliably credited with eighty-one duets.[12] Most of them are scored for two voices and continuo only, but six require additional (unspecified) instruments, for which the parts are lost. The commonest pairs of voices are soprano-alto, soprano-tenor, and soprano-bass, for each of which a similar number of works survives from his pen. The number of movements varies from one to six, and most of the works include a solo movement for each of the singers.

Apart from the later versions of the nineteen duets that he revised (all but one of which appear to have been finished between July and December 1702), only six of his duets can be precisely dated, and all of these are relatively late. Five were shown by Einstein to have been composed at Brussels between 1698 and 1700 for Sophie Charlotte, then electress of Brandenburg;[13] the other, *Dolce labbro, amabil bocca,* was almost certainly written for Antonio Pasi and Gaetano Berenstadt at Herten in the summer of 1712 or 1713.

It is clear, however, that Steffani was also composing duets during his Munich years. On 25 August 1693 the former Bavarian princess Violanta Beatrice asked him to send her some of those "duetti che si cantavano in Baviera alla Tavola" and cited an aria beginning "Crede ogn'un che sia pazzia,"[14] which turns out to be not a lost duet, as stated in *Die Musik in Geschichte und Gegenwart,* but the second verse of the soprano solo in the surviving duet *Oh! che voi direste bene.* Since Violanta Beatrice had moved to Florence in January 1689 as the bride of Grand-Prince Ferdinando of Tuscany, Steffani had almost certainly written *Oh! che voi direste bene* by the time he left Munich in 1688 and had probably composed some of the unnamed "duetti" that the princess desired.

Assuming that a given cantata text enjoyed only a brief period of popularity before falling out of favor, one can also find signs that Steffani wrote duets in the earliest stages of his composing career. His *Tu m'aspettasti al mare* is based on a text set as a solo cantata by Cesti, who died in 1669: Steffani presumably came across it in Rome between 1672 and 1674. *La fortuna su la ruota* is similarly based on a duet ascribed to Carlo Ambrogio Lonati, who also worked in Rome for several years, with Stradella. For the words and some of the musical material of *No, no, no, non voglio se devo amare*, Steffani drew on Carlo Donato Cossoni's *Cantate a una, due, e tre voci*, op. 13 [1671–79], and in *Dir che giovi* he used a text, a version of which was set as a solo cantata by Count Pirro Albergati and published at Bologna in 1687. These concordances appear to suggest that Steffani composed duets from the start of his career and that he was influenced by the cantata in Rome and Bologna.

Further insight toward a chronological perspective is sometimes afforded by knowledge of the poet or poetical source. The identity of the author is known in the case of only two of the duets in the present edition—*E perché non m'uccidete* and *E così mi compatite?* The texts of these were written by Brigida Bianchi and were published, together with that of one other Steffani duet, in her *Rifiuti di Pindo* (Paris: C. Chenault, 1666).[15] Bianchi worked for much of her life in Paris, as an actress and singer in the Comédie italienne (under the name Aurelia Fedeli), and these three texts are among a number that she described as intended for music. Since the only known settings of these texts are those of Steffani, he may have taken them directly from her book—presumably when he visited Paris in 1678–79. If this is so, he may have composed his settings during his visit—besides playing the harpsichord to Louis XIV and acquainting himself with the French style.

In view of what has already been said, it is hardly surprising that Steffani's texts seem typical of their period and genre. The only dialogue among his eighty-one chamber duets, *Io mi parto*, was written for a special occasion in 1700;[16] the other texts are monologues, only four of which include any narrative. The influence of the Arcadian movement is evident in some of them, but the majority are lyrical, amatory poems more typical of the cantata between 1660 and 1690. Although most of them are concerned with unrequited love, a number deal with love requited, jealousy, separation, or some such topic.

This limitation of subject-matter (and imagery) is compensated by the variety of meters and forms employed. The texts are composed of two kinds of verse—free verse (*versi sciolti*), using lines of seven and eleven syllables and deriving from the sixteenth-century madrigal, and arias, using lines with any number of syllables (eight is by far the most common) after the manner of Gabriello Chiabrera (1552–1638). In stanzas of free verse the lines need not be arranged in any pattern or display a regular rhyme-scheme; in arias, on the other hand, there is a pattern and a rhyme-scheme, and there may be two matching strophes. Unlike the stanzas in later cantatas, those set by Steffani often include both kinds of verse, and arias frequently end with an eleven-syllable line. Some of his texts consist entirely either of free verse or of arias, but most of them include one or two stanzas of each kind, ar-

ranged in one of a number of ways. Since free verse is set sometimes for both voices and sometimes as solo recitative, and arias may be set as solos or duets, the texts suggest, but by no means determine, the shape of the musical setting.

As far as overall musical form is concerned, the duets may be divided into three broad groups, which we may term madrigals, arias, and cantatas and which reflect the main kinds of Italian vocal chamber music in the seventeenth and early eighteenth centuries. The madrigals, some of which are based on texts consisting entirely of free—madrigalian—verse, are through-composed or "open" structures: none of the movements is repeated after any of the others. Most of the movements are also through-composed, though some include a repeat of a section (e.g., *Quanto care al cor voi siete*, p. 10 in this edition). The madrigals are set for both voices throughout and employ a range of styles and textures reminiscent of the form in the late Renaissance and early baroque.

Unlike the madrigals, the "aria" duets, which represent roughly half of the total, are closed structures employing a variety of forms created by repetition of a movement or large section. The repetition is normally prompted by a rhyme in the text. In these duets, standard *seicento* aria forms can be seen both in individual movements (solos and duets) and in the arrangement of movements in works as a whole.

Most of the "aria" duets are in da capo form, in which the first movement, invariably a duet, is repeated at the end. The intervening movements or sections may also be duets, as in *E perché non m'uccidete* (p. 34), but nearly always comprise a couple of solos. Although these sometimes employ recitative, they normally include, or consist entirely of, arias—some of them in extended forms such as ABBCDD, recalling Stradella's "aria pairs."[17] The solo arias are often strophic, but *Ribellatevi, o pensieri* (p. 20) and *Su, ferisci, alato arciero* (p. 26) are the only works in which the two strophes of an aria are given to different singers.

E così mi compatite? (p. 43) is one of five works in which the overall form is strophic, though since each strophe (exceptionally) includes a passage for one solo singer or the other, the music cannot be repeated exactly. *Pria ch'io faccia altrui palese* (p. 1) has a strophic text but is not set strophically: the second halves of the strophes are set to the same music, reflecting perhaps the refrain in the text, but the first halves are not. This is not the only work in which Steffani ignores a possibility offered by the text, and the resulting form (AB Cb) also occurs in a few other of his duets.

The remaining "aria" duets are either in rondo or strophic-rondo form. The rondos comprise three movements of which the first, a duet, is repeated after each of two solos (ABACA). In strophic-rondos the "episodes" are strophically related (ABAbA) and are also set mainly as duets, with built-in solo passages similar to those in *E così mi compatite?*

The "cantata" duets combine features of both the madrigals and the arias. Although they are open structures, they normally comprise two solo movements followed, and in most cases preceded, by a duet. The solo and duet movements serve a formal function similar to that of the recitatives and arias (respectively) in the late baroque solo cantata. The commonest pattern (duet, solo, solo, duet) can be seen in *Vorrei dire un non so che* (p. 79), *Occhi belli, non più* (p. 89), and *Begl'occhi, oh Dio, non più* (p. 103), but in *Aure, voi che volate* (p. 115) and others the order is solo, duet, solo, duet, and a few works dispense entirely with the first of the duets. *Saldi marmi, che coprite* (p. 51) is unique, however, in providing a solo for only one of the singers: this movement was added during Steffani's revision of his chamber duets, begun in 1702.

The solos in the "cantata" duets employ a rather distinctive form. While some of them are, or include, arias similar to those discussed above, the majority are recitatives in which the final line or couplet is set as a *cavata*—an extended section in arioso style, and in AA (or AA') form, which is the tonal complement of the recitative that it concludes. This kind of arioso section appears to have been a standard feature of the Italian cantata from the mid-seventeenth to the early eighteenth century. It occurs frequently in the works of Steffani's contemporaries, recalls a practice of Luigi Rossi, and foreshadows Albinoni's fugal "ariettas."[18] As one might expect, however, it is rare in Steffani's "aria" duets.

The style of Steffani's chamber duets, as well as the form, is based on the cantata of the mid-seventeenth century. He shares Carissimi's preference for minor keys and Cesti's for triple or compound meter, and his elegant melodies are laden with imagery typical of the genre at the time. Although his duets are tonally closed, they normally include at least one movement that begins in one key and ends in another, or is wholly in a related key. His harmony is enriched by an expressive use of chromaticism (e.g., *Begl'occhi, oh Dio, non più*, mvt. I, mm. 6–17 and 33–46; mvt. II, mm. 25–26) and a predilection for suspensions in the bass as well as the upper parts (e.g., *Pria ch'io faccia*, mvt. I, mm. 41 and 52; mvt. II, m. 8). In duet movements the continuo acts mainly as a harmonic support, though it occasionally imitates or anticipates a voice (e.g., *Vorrei dire*, mvt. I, mm. 1–2; *Saldi marmi*, mvt. I, mm. 1–14), especially between sections (e.g., *Ribellatevi, o pensieri*, mvt. I, m. 29); but in solo arias and *cavate* it often imitates the voice for longer periods or supports it with an ostinato or a "walking" bass (e.g., *Occhi belli, non più*, mvt. III).

These basic ingredients are joined by features of the French style and of the contemporary Italian trio sonata. The influence of French dance meters and dotted rhythms can be seen in duet and solo movements (e.g., *Su, ferisci, alato arciero*, mvt. II), and that of the trio sonata in the contrapuntal treatment of the voices in duets. These display a mastery of all the imitative textures used by his predecessors and of features, such as real and tonal answers, double counterpoint, and stretto, more typical of later instrumental fugues.

Steffani's developing interest and skill in counterpoint are particularly evident in his revised versions where, largely by exploring more thoroughly the contrapuntal potential of material recast for the purpose, he substantially increased the length and complexity of most of the duet movements. As if to compensate for this, some duet movements were reduced or excised, along with most of the solos. Compared with the earlier versions, the revi-

sions tend as a result of these changes to comprise a smaller number of larger movements of which a greater proportion are duets and are not repeated. The revisions can therefore be seen as a move away from the closed forms, involving repetition, so common in cantatas of the mid-seventeenth century, toward the open designs of the solo cantata and trio sonata of the later baroque. This move brought with it, paradoxically, a revival of interest in the madrigal, which perhaps afforded the greatest scope for formal expansion born of contrapuntal mastery. In these respects, and in the firmer grasp of tonal procedures that accompanies them, Steffani's works reflect—and he undoubtedly promoted—some of the most important developments in Italian music during the period in which he lived.

Sources

The earliest edition of a substantial selection of Steffani's duets is that prepared by Alfred Einstein and Adolf Sandberger and published in Denkmäler der Tonkunst in Bayern, vol. 11, Jahrgang 6/2 (Leipzig: Breitkopf & Härtel, 1905). It appears to be drawn from a number of sources and the selection is biased towards duets for soprano and alto and those without solo movements. The present edition, on the other hand, includes two groups of six duets, each in the order in which the composer left them, from two of the earliest and most authoritative sources that survive. It complements the DTB edition by favoring duets for two sopranos and those with solo movements, and it also gives a more accurate impression of the formal and stylistic range of Steffani's output in the genre.

The first six duets in the present edition have been edited from London, British Library, RM 23. k. 14. This is the second in a set of thirteen or more manuscript volumes which, despite the absence of any ascription, can almost certainly be identified with the new collection of chamber duets, including revised versions, that Steffani began to prepare in the autumn of 1702. Only eight of these volumes (RM 23. k. 13-20) are known to survive, and RM 23. k. 14 is one of two in the composer's hand (see Plate Ib) that were probably copied at Hanover by March 1703 and bound there by around 1710.[19] It comprises sixty-four folios of music paper in small oblong quarto. The pages measure approximately 22.75 by 17.25 cm and were numbered by the composer who, according to Einstein, also executed the charming miniatures for the initial letters of the six duets.[20]

The title of RM 23. k. 14 —"VETVSTATE RELICTA / DVETTI" (Plate Ia)—is slightly ambiguous, but the words "oldness having been abandoned" would seem to refer to the revision of the duets. Four of the works are certainly revisions of earlier versions, but *Su, ferisci, alato arciero* and *E così mi compatite?* are known only in the versions presented here and so do not appear to have been revised.

The second group of six duets in this edition is taken from British Library RM 23. k. 7. This is the first in a pair of manuscripts (RM 23. k. 7–8) apparently intended for Sophie Charlotte after she had become queen of Prussia in 1701. The title page (Plate IIa) bears a monogram composed of the letters "S" and "C," surmounted by a crown, and the title itself ("REGIA DIGNVM MODVLA-MEN AVRE / DVETTI / Del Sig:ʳ Abbate / De Steffani") may be translated "Duets: Music Worthy of a Royal Ear."

These latter manuscripts were probably copied shortly before 7 December 1702. In a letter of that date Steffani told Sophie Charlotte that "a couple of dozen" duets were ready for her[21]—among them, presumably, the majority of his revised versions. This pair of manuscripts originally contained twenty-six duets, including all but one of his nineteen known revisions; since the missing revision, *Torna a dar vita,* is also the only such work that is not to be found in either of the autographs mentioned above, it may have been finished too late for inclusion.

The manuscripts containing this second group of duets would appear to have been designed for use at a harpsichord and bound for shelving in a library. They are large oblong quarto volumes, sturdily bound in full leather with gold-stamped decoration on the covers. The music pages measure approximately 32 by 27 cm and are ruled with only six staves each. Since the duets were copied by a professional scribe in a large, clear hand, music and words can be read at a distance.

The first six duets in RM 23. k. 7 are the same as those in the autograph volume RM 23. k. 18 and are published in DTB. The next six probably correspond with the contents of one of the volumes now missing from RM 23. k. 13–20 and constitute the second group in the present edition. Except for *Ravvediti, mio core,* of which only this version is known, all these duets are revisions of earlier versions surviving elsewhere. As the index of RM 23. k. 7 makes clear, these twelve duets are all that the manuscript originally contained. A further duet, which cannot be attributed reliably to Steffani, was inserted at the end by a different hand at a later date. Einstein suggested that the text of this work (*Quando un eroe che s'ama*) refers to Prince Georg August of Hanover and his recruitment into Marlborough's army in 1708.[22]

It seems doubtful whether these manuscripts were ever given to Sophie Charlotte. If they had been, they would probably not be in London today, for her library passed to Princess Amalia, sister of Frederick the Great, and then to the Joachimsthal Hochschule. They may have been given instead to Caroline of Ansbach, Sophie's ward from 1696 and later queen of England, and they may be identical with the "Duetti del Sig:ʳ Abbate Steffani fol. 2 Vol." that are mentioned in a posthumous inventory of her library.[23] This possibility would seem to be strengthened by the fact that she married Georg August and moved to Hanover in 1705, the year of Sophie Charlotte's decease.

Editorial Methods

1. Incipit. The original clef, key signature, time signature, and first note of each part are shown in an incipit before the start of each piece.

2. Clefs. The soprano and alto clefs used for these voices in the sources have been replaced by the treble clef. The tenor clef has been replaced in the tenor part by the transposing treble clef and in the continuo part (*Occhi*

belli, non più, mvt. II, mm. 38–39 and 42–43, and mvt. III, m. 24) by the bass clef. The baritone clef, used for the bass voice (only) in *Aure, voi che volate,* has been replaced by the bass clef. These changes have been made without further comment.

3. Key signatures. The original signatures have been retained except in *Pria ch'io faccia, Saldi marmi,* and *Ravvediti, mio core,* where they have been modernized. None of the music has been transposed.

4. Accidentals. The notation of accidentals has been modernized. The following changes have been made tacitly: (a) a natural sign has occasionally been substituted for a sharp or a flat, as appropriate; (b) accidentals made redundant by the modern convention that an accidental remains in force until canceled by a barline or a further accidental have been omitted.

Editorial accidentals have been supplied in square brackets. When a note with no accidental in the source is inflected by an editorial key signature, the reading of the source is given in the Critical Notes. On the other hand, accidentals made necessary by some editorial action (*viz.,* modernization of the key signature, an earlier editorial accidental, or editorial barring) have been supplied tacitly, since they represent the reading of the source.

Cautionary accidentals have been added editorially in parentheses.

5. Time signatures and barring. In duple and quadruple time the original C and ₵ signatures have been retained. Triple or compound time is notated in the sources either (a) in C_4^3 or $\frac{3}{4}$ with six quarter-notes to the measure, or (b) in C_2^3 or $\frac{3}{2}$ with six half-notes to the measure; these signatures have been tacitly replaced by $\frac{6}{4}$ and $\frac{6}{2}$ respectively. Original note-values have been retained throughout, though tied notes in the sources have on occasion been rendered as a single note, and vice versa.

Where the barring in the sources is regular, it has been retained. Irregular barring has also been retained where necessary or desirable: in these cases, editorial time signatures have been added in square brackets. Elsewhere, irregular barring has been regularized and the barring in the sources has been described in the Critical Notes. Redundant barlines, which sometimes occur halfway through a measure without disturbing the regular barring pattern, have been omitted without comment.

6. Tempo indications. Two of the three tempo indications in the sources appear in conjunction with the continuo line; these have been tacitly moved to the appropriate place above the top staff of the system. Since the required tempo is usually fairly clear (movements barred in six should generally be felt in two), only a few editorial tempo indications ("recitativo" and "a tempo") have been added in square brackets. Where there is a change of time within the course of a movement, the relationship between the speeds of the two sections is expressed editorially by a metrical equivalent: [old value = new].

7. Continuo. With one exception, the original part consists of a single bass line only and is unfigured. The exception occurs in *Occhi belli, non più,* mvt. III, mm. 20–25, where the composer momentarily provides a second voice for the part. In this edition the original part appears throughout in regular notes in the lower staff of the continuo, while the editorial realization is notated in cue-size

notes mainly on the upper staff but sometimes also on the lower.

8. Repeats. The notation of repeats has been modernized in the following ways.

a. Double barlines with dots (𝄇) appear in the sources in four duets. In three cases they clearly denote the end of a section rather than the need for repeats and so have been relegated to description in the Critical Notes. In the second movement of *Su, ferisci, alato arciero*, however, they do appear to indicate repeats and have been retained in the musical text. Here Soprano I sings the whole of verse one followed by Soprano II with the whole of verse two.

b. Instructions calling for a repeat of the first movement or section appear at the end of three duets. Here the original wording has been placed in the Critical Notes and the modern equivalent supplied in the music in square brackets.

c. All other repeats indicated in the edition are fully written out in the sources. The attendant repeat signs and instructions, as well as the verse numbers, are therefore editorial. Discrepancies in the sources between the first and second statement of a repeated section are recorded in the Critical Notes.

9. Inscriptions. The designation "À 2" and the words "Segue" and "Fine," which frequently appear in RM 23. k. 7, have been tacitly suppressed. The abbreviation "2:ª" has been expanded and the indications "P:º Solo" and "2:º Solo" have been replaced by modern equivalents.

10. Ties. In the sources there are some notes—particularly pedal notes in the bass at the end of a system or page—that lack ties demanded by the musical sense. These ties have been editorially supplied as crossed ties (⌣).

11. Slurs. Slurs that are in the sources have generally been retained in the edition; the few that have been omitted have been recorded in the Critical Notes. Editorial slurs are shown as crossed (⌣): most of these have been supplied by analogy with slurs in the sources, but a few have been added to clarify the underlay.

In those repeated sections or movements that are written out twice in the sources but printed once in the edition, three kinds of slur have been used: the normally notated slurs appear in both statements of the passage in the source; crossed slurs appear in neither statement and are therefore editorial, while dotted slurs appear in one statement but not the other (the Critical Notes make clear which statement it is).

12. Indications for Performance. A wavy line (〰) occasionally appears above a voice part in RM 23. k. 7 (see Plate IIb). Although this resembles the contemporary sign for the slurred tremolo in string music,[24] its precise significance in Steffani's duets is not entirely clear.

Editorial appoggiaturas have been notated in two ways: Those in square brackets should be performed in the conventional manner before the following note, while stemless note-heads in parentheses should replace the following note—they indicate the pitch at which it may be sung, if taken as an appoggiatura.

Trills in square brackets are editorial.

13. Texts. Except for *E perché non m'uccidete* and *E così*

mi compatite?, for which Bianchi's *Rifiuti di Pindo* provides a complementary source, the texts have been edited entirely from the music manuscripts. The layout of the texts as presented below therefore reflects editorial understanding of their versification and poetical structure, but in most cases it also corresponds with the form of the musical setting.

The texts have been tacitly edited in the following ways. Orthography and spelling have generally been modernized, though a few unusual or archaic spellings have been retained for special reasons; the use of accents has also been modernized. The sparse original punctuation has been incorporated or modernized where appropriate, but most of the punctuation remains editorial. Initial capitals have been retained for titles, personifications, and proper names; they are supplied at the start of each line, but elsewhere suppressed. The underlay of the sources has been followed throughout, except in *Su, ferisci, alato arciero*, mvt. II, mm. 24–26, where bracketed type indicates an editorial substitution.

Notes on Performance

In Steffani's day his duets were performed by amateur and professional musicians at court and on stage. In Bavaria, as we have seen, they were sung "alla Tavola"; at Hanover they were performed by various ladies of the court. In Berlin Sophie Charlotte accompanied Bononcini and Ariosti[25] (did they transpose them down an octave?), while at Herten the castratos Pasi and Berenstadt were presumably accompanied by Steffani himself. Six "duetto's" were performed by Durastanti and Senesino at the King's Theatre, Haymarket, in 1721,[26] and Mrs. Arne assured Burney that Senesino and Strada often sang them during their morning studies.[27]

The duets are still suitable for domestic and concert use today. Because of the contrapuntal texture of the parts, they are best performed by the voices for which they are scored, although works for two sopranos could perhaps be sung by two tenors. Most of the duets can be tackled by amateur singers, provided, as Mattheson says, they are "secure in the saddle,"[28] but a few (e.g., *Occhi belli, non più* and *Aure, voi che volate*) demand a virtuoso technique.

Although there is room for ornamentation in the solo movements, little is possible or needed in the duets, even in repeats, beyond an occasional appoggiatura or trill. Tosi once heard, or dreamed of hearing, "a famous *Duetto* torn into Atoms by two renown'd Singers, in Emulation; the one proposing, and the other by Turns answering, that at last it ended in a Contest, who could produce the most Extravagancies." When translating this passage, Galliard added that the "Abott *Steffani*, so famous for his *Duetto's*, would never suffer such luxuriant Singers to perform any of them, unless they kept themselves within Bounds."[29] Since, according to Hawkins,[30] Galliard was a pupil of Steffani, he presumably knew what he was talking about.

Although at that time the continuo part may have been played on either a bass stringed instrument or a harpsichord, the voices are better supported if both kinds of instrument are used. The harpsichordist should remember that he is an accompanist, not a soloist. A major source of delight in these duets is the variety of harmonic and contrapuntal effects created within the vocal parts and between them and the bass; these effects should not be obscured by extraneous activity at the keyboard.

Critical Notes

The readings in the edition are identical to those in the sources except in the particulars noted below. Reference is made to the movement, measure, part, and note or beat. In arriving at the number of a note at issue, editorial appoggiaturas are ignored, but all tied notes are counted separately. The following abbreviations are used: S = Soprano (SI = Soprano I, and SII = Soprano II, as necessary); A = Alto; T = Tenor; B = Bass; Bc = Basso continuo. The traditional system of pitch designation is used, wherein middle C = c', the octave above is c'', etc.

Pria ch'io faccia altrui palese

Mvt. I. Mm. 22–23: double barline with dots. M. 28, Bc, notes 1–2: tied. M. 35, SII, beats 1–3: dotted whole-note, no half-rest. M. 57, all parts: notes lack dot.

Mvt. II. Headed "2:a." M. 10, SI, note 6: eighth-note. M. 13, Bc, note 3: f-sharp. M. 16, SI, note 2: eighth-note; SII, note 5: eighth-note. Mm. 26–27: double barline with dots. M. 62, all parts: notes lack dot.

Quanto care al cor voi siete

Mvt. I. M. 3, SI, notes 6–7: no slur second time. M. 11, Bc, note 3: a (first time).

Mvt. II. M. 15: double barline with dots. Mm. 37–38: no barline.

Mvt. III. M. 13: extra barline halfway through the measure, followed by regular barring (in six) to the end of the piece. M. 61, all parts: notes lack dot.

Ribellatevi, o pensieri

Mvt. I. M. 18, SII, notes 7–8: no slur second time. M. 20, SI, notes 7–8: no slur first time. M. 24, Bc, note 2: B (first time). M. 28, SII, notes 4–5: no slur first time. M. 30, all parts: dotted half-note.

Mvt. II. First verse headed "P:° Solo," second verse "2:° Solo." In the source the movement is barred regularly in six from the start, yielding a half-measure at the end (there are barlines halfway through, and at the end of, m. 28). M. 2, S, notes 5–6: no slur in verse 1. M. 3, S, notes 6–7: no slur in verse 1. M. 8, S, notes 2–3: no slur in verse 1. M. 14: double barline with dots. This could denote a repeat of the first half of the movement, in both verses, but not of the second half: the way in which the end of verse 1 is dovetailed in the source with the start of verse 2, and the absence of dots at the final double bar, rule out the possibility of such a repeat. M. 15, S, notes 2–4: no slur in verse 1. M. 16, S, notes 2–4: no slur in verse 1. M. 17, S, notes 6–8: no slur in verse 1. M. 18, S, notes 6–8: no slur in verse 2. M. 27, S, notes 4–5: no slur in verse 2.

M. 29: final repeat instruction reads "Ribellatevi, o pensieri ij / Da Capo."

Su, ferisci, alato arciero

Mvt. I. M. 38, Bc: note one is two dotted half-notes. M. 84, all parts: dotted half-note.

Mvt. II. First verse headed "P:° Solo," second verse "2:° Solo." M. 6, S, notes 2–3: no slur in verse 1. M. 13, S, notes 3–4: no slur in verse 1. M. 24, S, notes 3–4: no slur in verse 2. Mm. 24–26, SI (verse 1): text reads "Porta seco La speranza." The editorial underlay makes better grammatical sense, corresponds with the underlay of verse 2, and justifies the musical relationship between the last two phrases of the movement. M. 25, S, notes 2–3 and 5–6: no slurs in verse 2. M. 28, S, notes 5–6: no slur in verse 2. M. 29, S, notes 2–3: no slur in verse 2. M. 31: final repeat instruction reads "Su, ferisci ij / Da Capo."

E perché non m'uccidete

The text is entitled "Occhi crudeli" in Bianchi's *Rifiuti di Pindo*, pp. 123-24. Between lines 8 and 9 Bianchi includes the following five additional lines: E perche &c. / Morte mi fora / Pena men ria, / Che gelosia / Soffrir ogn'hora. Steffani included these lines in an earlier setting of the poem (Bologna, Civico Museo Bibliografico Musicale, MS V. 195, ff.58r–61r) but omitted them from the revised version presented in this edition.

M. 19, S, note 3: lacks dot; T, notes 2 and 7: lack dot. M. 20, S, note 2: lacks dot. M. 29, S, notes 1–3: slur. M. 55, all parts: notes lack dot. Mm. 56–57, S and T: "mancar" for "mancan." M. 76: extra barline halfway through the measure, followed by regular barring (in four) until m. 81. M. 81, all parts: quarter-rest without fermata is followed by half-rest with fermata. M. 109: final repeat instruction reads "E perche non m'uccidete ij / Da Capo."

E così mi compatite?

The text is entitled "Occhi crudeli" in Bianchi's *Rifiuti di Pindo*, pp. 133–34.

M. 4, S, notes 2–3: no slur in verse 1. M. 11, S, notes 2–4: slur in verse 2; note 4: sharp lacking in verse 1. M. 12: extra barline halfway through the measure in verse 1, followed by regular barring (in six). M. 17, S, notes 5–6: no slur in verse 1. M. 18, T, notes 2–3: two quarter-notes in verse 2; notes 5–6: no slur in verse 1. M. 22, T, note 3: two quarter-notes, lacking tie, in verse 1. M. 25: extra barline halfway through the measure in verse 2, followed by regular barring (in six); Bc, note 2: B in verse 1. M. 26, T, note 4: no natural, though in same measure as preceding d'-sharp. M. 31, S, notes 3–4: no slur in verse 2. M. 72, all parts: dotted half-note.

Saldi marmi, che coprite

Mvt. I. M. 23, SI, note 2: lacks flat. M. 34, SI, note 5: lacks flat. M. 44, SII, notes 2–3: slur. M. 65: the barline at the end of the measure occurs halfway through the next measure and is followed by regular barring (in six) to the end of the movement. M. 74, all parts: dotted whole-note.

Mvt. III. M. 20, Bc, note 2: F. M. 26, SI, note 3: flat. M. 38, SI, note 2: lacks flat. M. 46, SII, notes 1–2: undotted half-note.

Mvt. IV. M. 10, SI, notes 1–2: slur. M. 28, SI, note 1: lacks flat. M. 30: extra barline halfway through the measure, followed by regular barring (in six) until m. 43, which has barlines in the middle and at the end. Mm. 52–53: barline in the middle of each measure but not between them. M. 55, Bc, note 2: tied to next note. M. 64, SI, notes 2–3: slur.

Ravvediti, mio core

Mvt. I. M. 7, SI, notes 2 and 3: lack flat. M. 15: the barline at the end of the measure occurs halfway through the next measure and is followed by regular barring (in six) to the end of the movement.

Mvt. III. Headed "2:ª Parte." M. 4, SI, note 10: f'. M. 6, SII, notes 4 and 7: lack flat. M. 8, SI, notes 4 and 7: lack flat.

Vorrei dire un non so che

Mvt. II. M. 22, Bc, note 1: A.

Mvt. III. M. 26, both parts: dotted whole-note.

Mvt. IV. M. 2, S, notes 5–6, and m. 3, T, notes 5–6: slurs appear under notes 4–5. M. 22: extra barline halfway through the measure, followed by regular barring (in six) to the end of the piece. M. 28, S, notes 2–3: slur. M. 57, all parts: dotted whole-note.

Occhi belli, non più

Mvt. I. M. 36, Bc, note 2: G. M. 43: extra barline halfway through the measure, followed by regular barring (in six) to the end of the movement. Mm. 46 and 53, S, and m. 53, T: "perche" for "perch'io."

Mvt. II. M. 16, S, note 7: e'.

Mvt. IV. M. 5, Bc, note 4: eighth-note. M. 5: the barline at the end of the measure occurs halfway through the next measure and is followed by regular barring (in six) until m. 15, which lacks the initial barline and is in effect a 9/4 measure. M. 8, T, beats 1–3: dotted whole-note, no rest. M. 9, T, beats 1–3: undotted whole-note followed by half-rest. M. 48, T, beats 4–6: dotted whole-note, no rest.

Begl'occhi, oh Dio, non più

Mvt. I. Mm. 48–49: barline halfway through each measure but not between them. M. 50, all parts: dotted whole-note.

Mvt. II. M. 11, Bc: dotted whole-note. M. 35, both parts: dotted whole-note.

Mvt. III. M. 2: "parto" for "parte."

Mvt. IV. M. 9, A, note 1: carries syllable "-ma" which belongs in next measure. M. 10, A: dotted double whole-note, with no half-rests, tied from previous note. Mm. 31–55: the rhythm ♩♩♪ is notated (a) as ♩. ♪ in mm. 31–32, A; 34–35, S; 39–40, A; 43–44, S; 46–47, A; 51, S; and (b) as ♩. ♩ or ♩♩ ♩ in mm. 36–37, S; 40, S; 51–52, A; 54–55, S; and 55, A.

Aure, voi che volate

Mvt. I. M. 9, B, note 12: sixteenth-note.

Mvt. II. M. 11, B, notes 2–3: dotted eighth-note with sixteenth-note (second time). M. 33, Bc, note 3: notated as g, but letter "f" written in different hand underneath.

Mvt. III. M. 6, A, note 4: thirty-second-note. M. 7, A, notes 10–11: sixteenth-notes. M. 21, both parts: dotted half-note.

Mvt. IV. M. 2, A, notes 3–4 and 8–9: no slurs first time. M. 3, Bc, notes 5–6: quarter-note a (second time). M. 4, A, notes 2–3 and 7–8: no slurs second time. M. 7, A, notes 6–7: no slur first time. M. 22, Bc, note 5: G.

Acknowledgments

I should like to thank Oliver Neighbour and his staff in the Music Library, British Library, for their kind assistance during the preparation of this edition, and Gerry Slowey, of the Italian Department of Birmingham University, for his help in editing and translating the texts. The editor and publisher are grateful to the British Library for permission to use the sources for this edition and to include reproductions from them.

Colin Timms

Notes

1. P. Keppler, "Agostino Steffani's Hannover Operas and a Rediscovered Catalogue," in *Studies in Music History: Essays for Oliver Strunk,* ed. H. Powers (Princeton: Princeton University Press, 1968), 341–54.

2. C. Timms, "Revisions in Steffani's Chamber Duets," *Proceedings of the Royal Musical Association* 96 (1969–70): 119–21.

3. G. Croll, "Zur Chronologie der 'Düsseldorfer' Opern Agostino Steffanis," in *Festschrift K. G. Fellerer zum 60. Geburtstag,* ed. H. Hüschen (Regensburg: Gustav Bosse, 1962), 82–87.

4. C. Timms, "Steffani and the Academy of Ancient Music," *Musical Times* 119 (1978): 127–30.

5. D. L. Burrows, preface to his edition of *Antonio Cesti, Four Chamber Duets,* Collegium Musicum: Yale University, 2nd ser., vol. 1 (Madison: A-R Editions, 1969), vii.

6. I am grateful to John Whenham for his help in formulating (and permission to quote) this definition, which is to be used in our joint book on the Italian cantata, currently in preparation.

7. The standard account is E. Schmitz, "Zur Geschichte des italienischen Kammerduetts im 17. Jahrhundert," *Jahrbuch der Musikbibliothek Peters* 23 (1916): 43–60.

8. W. Klenz, *Giovanni Maria Bononcini of Modena: A Chapter in Baroque Instrumental Music* (Durham, N. C.: Duke University Press, 1962), 141.

9. C. Burney, *A General History of Music* (London: printed for the author, 1776–89), 3:534.

10. E. Schmitz, "Zur Geschichte," 48–49.

11. C. Timms, "Handel and Steffani: A New Handel Signature," *Musical Times* 114 (1973): 374–77.

12. Unless otherwise stated, information about Steffani's duets is taken from my thesis, "The Chamber Duets of Agostino Steffani (1654–1728), with Transcriptions and Catalogue" (Ph.D. diss., University of London, 1977). Selections of duets appear in Denkmäler der Tonkunst in Bayern, vol. 11, Jahrgang 6/2 (Leipzig: Breitkopf & Härtel, 1905) and, in facsimile, in *Cantatas by Agostino Steffani 1654–1728,* selected and introduced by Colin Timms: The Italian Cantata in the Seventeenth Century, vol. 15 (New York: Garland Publishing Inc., 1985).

13. A. Einstein, "Die Briefe der Königin Sophie Charlotte und der Kurfürstin Sophie an Agostino Steffani," *Zeitschrift der internationalen Musikgesellschaft* 8 (1906–7): 86–87.

14. This letter and others are printed in J. Loschelder, "Aus Düsseldorfs italienischer Zeit: römische Quellen zu Agostino Steffanis Leben," *Beiträge zur rheinischen Musikgeschichte* 1 (Cologne, 1952): 38 and A. Della Corte, "Qualche lettera e qualche melodramma di Agostino Steffani," *Rassegna musicale* 32 (1962): 28.

15. The third Steffani duet based on a poem in Bianchi's *Rifiuti di Pindo* is *Sia maledetto Amor.* The texts of three others appeared in her *L'inganno fortunato . . . comedia bellissima . . . con alcune poesie musicali* (Paris: Claudio Cramoisy, 1659). Bianchi therefore wrote more of Steffani's texts than did any other poet whose work can be reliably identified.

16. A. Einstein, "Die Briefe der Königin Sophie Charlotte," 86–87.

17. O. Jander, "Alessandro Stradella and His Minor Dramatic Works" (Ph.D. diss., Harvard University, 1962), 226–38.

18. E. Caluori, "The Cantatas of Luigi Rossi" (Ph.D. diss., Brandeis University, 1971), 1:199; M. Talbot, preface to his edition of *Tomaso Albinoni, Twelve Cantatas Opus 4,* Recent Researches in the Music of the Baroque Era, vol. 31 (Madison: A-R Editions, 1979), viii.

19. For further information on the genesis of this collection see C. Timms, "Gregorio Piva and Steffani's Principal Copyist," *Source Materials and the Interpretation of Music: A Memorial Volume to Thurston Dart,* ed. Ian Bent (London: Stainer & Bell, 1981), 172–84. The contents of the other autograph (RM 23. k. 18) are published in Denkmäler der Tonkunst in Bayern, vol. 11, Jahrgang 6/2, 77–112.

20. DTB, vol. 11, Jahrgang 6/2, xii.

21. A. Ebert, "Briefe Agostino Steffanis an die Königin Sophie Charlotte von Preussen," *Die Musik* 6 (1906–7): 171.

22. DTB, vol. 11, Jahrgang 6/2, xiii.

23. *A Catalogue of the Royal Library of her late Majesty Queen Caroline. Distributed into Faculties. 1743* (MS, Windsor Castle), 177.

24. D. D. Boyden, *The History of Violin Playing from Its Origins to 1761* (London: Oxford University Press, 1965), 266–68.

25. A. Ebert, "Briefe Agostino Steffanis," 162.

26. O. E. Deutsch, *Handel: A Documentary Biography* (London: Adam and Charles Black, 1955), 127–28.

27. C. Burney, *A General History of Music,* 3:535–36.

28. J. Mattheson, *Der vollkommene Capellmeister* (Hamburg: C. Herold, 1739), 215.

29. P. F. Tosi, *Opinioni de' cantori antichi e moderni* (Bologna: L. dalla Volpe, 1723), trans. J. E. Galliard, *Observations on the Florid Song* (London: J. Wilcox, 1742), 150–51. Galliard omits Tosi's cautionary words "or dreamed of hearing."

30. J. Hawkins, *A General History of the Science and Practice of Music* (London: Payne and Son, 1776), 5:187, note.

Texts and Translations

Pria ch'io faccia altrui palese

Pria ch'io faccia altrui palese
Chi mi tien fra lacci stretto,
Di mia man con giuste offese
Mi trarrò l'alma dal petto.
   Vuò morire,
   Pria che dire
La cagion del mio desio:
Basta ben che lo sappia Amore ed io.

Ch'io riveli quello strale
Che lasciò l'alma ferita,
Nel mio duol, benché mortale,
Voglio perdere la vita.
   Cheto, cheto,
   Ma secreto,
Spererò quel che desio:
Basta ben che lo sappia Amore ed io.

Before I tell anybody
who it is that holds me tightly ensnared,
with my own hand, and committing no crime,
I will wrench my heart from my breast.
   I will die
   before I reveal
the cause of my desire:
enough that it is known by Cupid and me.

Before I name the dart
that wounded my heart,
in my suffering, though it be fatal,
I will forfeit my life.
   Quietly, quietly,
   but secretly,
I shall hope for that which I desire:
enough that it is known by Cupid and me.

Quanto care al cor voi siete

Quanto care al cor voi siete,
Mie catene,
Per colei che mi legò;
Amo sì fra voi le pene,
Che se mai non vi rompete
Io già mai non vi sciorrò.
Quanto care al cor voi siete,
Mie catene,
Per colei che mi legò.

Adorati miei tormenti,
Sì, stringetemi ogn'or più;
Che goder veri contenti
Non sa un cor che in voi non fu.
Mai, mai non v'allentate:
Che viver non poss'io se mi lasciate.

Vivi dunque incatenato,
O mio cor, sino alla morte;
E se all'ora il laccio forte
Eternarsi non potrà,
Per pietà de la mia doglia
La man che mi legò, quella mi scioglia.

How dear to my heart are you,
my chains,
because of her that tied you round me;
I love so much the pains you inflict,
that if you never break,
I shall never loose you.
How dear to my heart are you,
my chains,
because of her that tied you round me.

O my beloved torments,
yes, oppress me ever more;
a heart that has not experienced
suffering cannot enjoy true happiness.
Never, never let go:
I cannot live if you abandon me.

And so live on in chains,
my heart, until you die;
and if the powerful bond
cannot last for ever,
out of pity for my suffering
let the hand that bound me, then, free me.

Ribellatevi, o pensieri

Ribellatevi, o pensieri,
Pera il Dio d'Amor!
   A forza di sdegno
   Sovvertasi 'l regno,
   S'uccida 'l tiranno
   Che sempre d'affanno
   Nodrisce 'l mio cor.
Ribellatevi, o pensieri,
Pera il Dio d'Amor!

Rebel, o thoughts,
perish the God of Love!
   By force of disdain
   let his reign be overthrown;
   let the tyrant be killed
   who continually nourishes
   my heart with pain.
Rebel, o thoughts,
perish the God of Love!

Se perdei per infida bellezza,
Stolto amante, la mia libertà,
Frenesia così ria
Omai cangisi 'n furor.

Di schernirmi hai finito, Cupido,
Falso nume, bambino crudel;
Del tuo foco prendo a gioco
Il chimerico splendor.

Ribellatevi &c.

Su, ferisci, alato arciero

Su, ferisci, alato arciero,
Il tuo stral non fa morir.
Occhio nero che saetta
Fa una piaga che diletta
E fa dolce anco il martir.
Su, ferisci, alato arciero,
Il tuo stral non fa morir.

Che tormento può dar un guardo
Che s'incontra con piacer?
Fera pur il nume cieco,
Se 'l suo dardo
Porta seco
La speranza di goder.

Qual martire può dar quel seno
In cui fisso sta 'l desir?
Poca nube è quel tormento,
Ch'il sereno
D'un contento
In brev'ora fa sparir.

Su, ferisci &c.

E perché non m'uccidete   (Brigida Bianchi)

E perché non m'uccidete,
Spietatissimi occhi ingrati,
Se a' miei danni congiurati
Ch'io languisca risolvete?
E perché non m'uccidete?
Forse vi mancan l'armi
Per ferir, per piagarmi?
Ah no, che d'arco e strali armati siete.
Deh, luci amate,
Se negate
D'essere amiche stelle,
Siatemi pur rubelle,
Siatemi pur comete.
E perché &c.

E così mi compatite?   (Brigida Bianchi)

E così mi compatite?
Che mi giova, o luci ingrate,
Di servir se mi sprezzate,
Di languir se mi schernite?
E così mi compatite?
Io vi mostro un cor piagato
Per destare in voi pietà,
E voi, tutte crudeltà,
Perch'io mora disperato,

If I through your faithless beauty,
foolish lover, have lost my liberty,
let my miscreant passion
now change to fury.

You have ceased to deride me, Cupid,
false god, cruel boy;
I laugh
at the illusory splendor of your fire.

Rebel &c.

Come on, shoot, winged archer,
your dart does not kill.
A dark eye firing arrows of love
makes a wound that delights
and a pain that also is sweet.
Come on, shoot, winged archer,
your dart does not kill.

What suffering can be given by a glance
that is met with delight?
Then let the blind god strike,
if his arrow
brings with it
the hope of pleasure.

What torment can be caused by that heart
in which desire is fixed?
That torment is a slender cloud,
which by the clear sky
of one delight
is quickly dispelled.

Come on, shoot &c.

And why do you not kill me,
most pitiless, ungrateful eyes,
if, dedicated to my downfall,
you resolve that I should pine?
And why do you not kill me?
Perhaps you lack the weapons
with which to wound and injure me?
Ah, no, for you are armed with bow and arrows.
Come, beloved eyes,
if you refuse
to be propitious stars,
be hostile, then,
be comets of doom.
And why &c.

Is this how you pity me?
What use is it to me, o ungrateful eyes,
to serve if you despise me,
to pine if you deride me?
Is this how you pity me?
I show you a wounded heart
to awaken pity in you,
and you, unmitigated cruelty,
so that I may die in despair,

Mi squarciate le ferite.
E così mi compatite?

E così mi consolate?
  Per conforto del mio duolo
  Io vi chiedo un guardo solo
  E voi crude me 'l negate.
E così mi consolate?
  Io di pianto aspergo il ciglio,
  Additandovi il mio ardor,
  E voi, colme di rigor,
  Minacciando aspro periglio,
  L'alma mia più tormentate.
E così mi consolate?

Saldi marmi, che coprite

  "Saldi marmi, che coprite
  Del mio ben l'ignuda salma,
  Ch'ogni dì più in mezz'all'alma
  La mia fede stabilite,
  Che ne dite?
  Deggio al nuovo desire
  Opporre il vostro gelo, o pur morire?"
Così Fille dicea,
Del suo perduto bene
Rivolta un giorno alle bellezze estinte.
Viss'ella di Fileno
Lunga stagione in fortunati amori;
Ma già le bionde ariste
Quattro volte divise avea dal suolo
Del curvo mietitor la falce adunca
Da ch'ei, cedendo a morte,
Tra solitarii ardor lasciolla in vita;
Non vantâr mai, tra tanto,
Lacci un crin, risi un labbro,
O strali un ciglio, onde il suo cor fedele
O piagato, o invaghito, o avvinto fosse.
Mostrolle al fine il caso
Ne' begl'occhi di Tirsi
Dell'amato Filen mille sembianze;
Onde, fatta incapace
Di resister al bel ch'amò una volta,
Risoluta d'amare ancora un dì,
Parlando a' pensier suoi, disse così:

  "Incostanza, e che pretendi?
  Amerò, sì, ch'amerò.
  So ben io come si può
  Cangiar amanti e non cangiar gl'incendi.

  "Voi tra tanto, occhi lucenti,
  Che nel cor mi ravvivate
  Quegl'ardor ch'eran già spenti,
  Consolate i miei tormenti,
  Ch'altri per voi, e voi per altri adoro;
  Vissi agl'estinti, e per chi vive or moro."

Ravvediti, mio core

  Ravvediti, mio core.
  Tante lagrime,
  Tanti gemiti,
  A che giovano

tear open my wounds.
Is this how you pity me?

Is this how you console me?
  For the relief of my pain
  I ask of you a single glance,
  and you, pitiless, deny it to me.
Is this how you console me?
  My eyes are wet with tears,
  thus showing you my love,
  and you, full of coldness,
  threatening terrible disaster,
  torment my heart still further.
Is this how you console me?

  "O solid marble slabs that cover
  the naked corpse of my beloved,
  that day by day confirm my love
  more deeply in my heart,
  what have you to say?
  Must I oppose this new desire
  with your coldness, or die?"
Thus said Phyllis
when she turned one day
to the dead beauties of her lost love.
She had lived for a long time,
happy in the love of Philenus,
but the golden ears of corn had already
been severed from the ground four times
by the curved sickle of the hunched reaper
since he, succumbing to death,
had left her alive with her lonely passion.
Meanwhile, no tresses could boast
of fetters, no lips of laughter,
no eyes of darts by which her faithful heart
had been wounded, charmed, or bound.
At length chance showed her
in the beautiful eyes of Thyrsis
a thousand features of her beloved Philenus;
and so, unable to resist
the beauty she once had loved,
and determined to love again one day,
talking to her thoughts, she said:

  "Inconstancy, what do you want?
  I shall love again, yes, I shall love.
  I know very well how one can
  change lovers but not change the fires.

  "You, meanwhile, bright eyes,
  that revive in my heart
  those passions that once were dead,
  console my torments, for I love another
  because of you and you because of another;
  I lived for the dead, and now for one who lives I die."

  Think hard, my heart.
  All this weeping,
  all this sobbing—
  what use is it

Se i sospiri,
Se i martiri,
Servon solo ad accrescerti il dolore?
Ravvediti, mio core.

Non han forza i miei lamenti
D'impetrar pietosa aita;
È cagion de' miei tormenti
Sol colei che chiami vita.

S'a morire mi condanna
Il tuo barbaro rigore,
Che pretendi dal mio core,
Adorata mia tiranna?
   Le mie pene,
   Le catene,
   Prendi a gioco,
   Ed ardi al pianto mio, geli al mio foco.

if the sighs
and the torments
serve only to increase your sorrow?
Think hard, my heart.

My laments have no power
to elicit merciful help;
the sole cause of my torments
is she whom you call your life.

If your cruel coldness
condemns me to die,
what do you require from my heart,
my beloved tyrant?
   My pains,
   my chains,
   you laugh at them,
   and you burn at my weeping and freeze at my burning.

Vorrei dire un non so che

   Vorrei dire un non so che,
   Che mi tiene oppresso il cor;
   Ma la lingua m'annoda Amor,
   Né conoscer so perché.

Udiste mai più strano caso, o bella?
So che voi sola siete
Cagion del mio martire,
E non ve lo so dire.
Cieco Amor si servì de' vostri lumi
Per far ch'io mi consumi,
E la sua crudeltà tanto s'estende
Che quando io son con voi muto mi rende.

Quando lontan da voi
Passo misere l'ore,
M'esce per gl'occhi il foco, ch'ho nel core
Stravaganze d'amore.
Quand'io vi son vicino,
Languisco, peno, moro;
Ma non vi saprei dir, bella, v'adoro.

   Quante volte mi propongo
   Palesarvi la mia fe'!
   Quante volte mi dispongo
   A voler chieder mercè!
   Ma che pro,
   Se già so
   Che sospiro e peno in vano
   Perché gelo vicino, ardo lontano?

   I'd like to tell you something or other
   which is pressing on my heart,
   but Cupid has tied my tongue,
   and I cannot find out why.

Did you ever hear a stranger tale, my love?
I know that you alone are
the cause of my suffering,
and I don't know how to tell you.
Blind Cupid used your eyes
to have me consumed,
and his cruelty extends so far
that when I am with you I am dumb.

When far from you,
I spend my time in misery;
fire burns in my eyes, for I have in my heart
the wild passions of love.
When close to you,
I languish, suffer, and die,
but I could never say, my love, I adore you.

   How often I propose
   to declare my love to you!
   How often I prepare myself
   to beg you for mercy!
   But what is the point,
   if I know already
   that I sigh and suffer in vain,
   because I freeze when near and burn far away?

Occhi belli, non più

Occhi belli, non più.
Voi siete vincitori, ed io son vinto:
Sono vinto ed avvinto.
Deh, posate, omai, posate,
Deh, non più saettate,
Perch'io trafitto moro
E moribondo i miei nemici adoro.

Renditi, omai, mio core,
E lascia la battaglia, or che non puoi
Resister contro doi.

Beautiful eyes, no more.
You are the victors and I am vanquished;
I am vanquished and enchained.
Come, leave off now, leave off,
come, strike no more,
because I, transfixed, am dying,
and in dying I worship my enemies.

Surrender now, my heart,
and give up the fight, since you can
no longer hold out against two foes.

Ceda, ceda il coraggio,
Hai troppo disvantaggio;
Pugnar fora un aborto
Contro doppio nemico un semimorto.

Perché, lumi bugiardi,
Offrirmi pace e poi mancar di fede?
Fermezza non si vede
In voi, mie stelle erranti,
Comete degl'amanti.
Begl'occhi mentitori,
Fe' non potete aver, nasceste mori.

Occhi, pietà, pietà.
Tanto crudeli più, quanto più belli.
Siete nati gemelli
Per duplicarmi affanni,
Solo uniti a' miei danni.
Già cado morto al suolo;
Voi per la morte mia vestite a duolo.

Let your courage give way,
your forces are too few;
it would be a disaster to fight
as a dying man against a double enemy.

Why, deceitful eyes,
offer me peace then go back on your word?
There is no constancy
in you, my wayward stars,
lovers' comets of doom.
Beautiful, mendacious eyes,
you cannot be trusted; you were born infidels.

Eyes, have mercy, have mercy!
The more beautiful you are, the more cruel.
You were born twins
to double my pains
and are united only for my affliction.
Already I fall dead to the ground;
you, since I die, dress yourself in mourning.

Begl'occhi, oh Dio, non più

Begl'occhi, oh Dio, non più,
Più non piangete, oh Dio,
Che per barbaro rigor
Del tiranno Dio d'Amor
Serve d'esca quell'acqua al foco mio.

Clori mia, s'il cor t'ingombra
Qualche dubbio di mia fe',
Tal pensier sgombra da te.
Per te, mia vita, moro;
Per te, mio ben, languisco.
Ma perché tu non miri
Quanto t'adoro, quanto?
Cieca ti rende il pianto,
Onde se, perché l'ami,
Col lagrimar tormenti un cor fedele,
La tua troppo pietà ti fa crudele.

Se la tua gelosia
È parte del tuo amor, o bella Clori,
Che fia dunque? Quando de' miei dolori
Dovrò sperare il fin? Mentre conviene
Che, perché troppo m'ami, io viva in pene.

Clori mia, deh, ferma alquanto,
Ferma il corso a quei due fiumi
Che dai lumi versi ogn'or;
Altrimente, o sorte ria,
In un mar d'amaro pianto
Vuoi sommerger il mio cor.

Beautiful eyes, O God, no more,
weep no more, O God,
for by barbarous decree
of the tyrannical God of Love,
those tears serve only to fuel my fire.

My Chloris, if your heart is burdened
with some doubt as to my fidelity,
put such thoughts behind you.
For you, my life, I die;
for you, my love, I pine.
But why do you not see
how much, how much I love you?
You are blinded by your tears
so that if, because you love a faithful heart,
you torment it with your weeping,
your excessive pity makes you cruel.

If your jealousy
is part of your love, o beautiful Chloris,
what then will happen? How long must I wait
for an end to my suffering? Meanwhile,
since you love me too much, I must live in pain.

My Chloris, pray, stop for a while,
stop the flow of those two streams
that you endlessly shed from your eyes.
Otherwise, o horrid fate,
in a sea of bitter tears
you will drown my heart.

Aure, voi che volate

Aure, voi che volate
D'intorno all'idol mio,
Per pietà li ridite il mio tormento;
E se non posso, oh Dio,
Provar questo contento,
Ch'oda da me 'l mio duol, voi glie'l narrate,
Zeffiretti cortesi, aurette grate:

Dite a Filli ch'io mi moro,
E m'uccide il suo rigor.

Breezes, you that waft
around my idol,
for pity's sake tell her of my torment;
and if I cannot, o God,
have the satisfaction
of telling her myself of my grief, you tell her,
courteous little Zephyrs, gracious little breezes:

Tell Phyllis that I am dying
and her coldness is the cause.

Più la speme non m'avviva,
Di conforto l'alma è priva;
Giunge tardi ogni ristoro,
Cado vittima al dolor.
Dite a Filli ch'io mi moro,
E m'uccide il suo rigor.

Diteli che per lei . . . ma no, tacete.
Nel vostro mormorio
Li sussurri all'orecchio il dolor mio.
Pur se parlar volete
Alla bella crudel che mi ferì,
Li direte così:

"Quando mai avrà mercè
Una lunga servitù?
Se pirausta innamorato
Mi nodrisco nel mio ardor,
Mai farammi un dì beato
Con sua face il Dio d'Amor;
E sperar non dovrò più
Se costante è la mia fe'.
Quando mai avrà mercè
Una lunga servitù?"

No more does hope revive me,
my heart can find no solace;
all succor comes too late,
I fall a victim to sorrow.
Tell Phyllis that I am dying
and her coldness is the cause.

Tell her that for her . . . but no, wait.
In your murmuring
whisper my sorrow into her ear.
Then if you wish to speak
to the cruel beauty who wounded me,
address her thus:

"When will you ever reward
my lengthy servitude?
If like an infatuated moth
I feed on my ardor,
the God of Love with his flaming torch
will never give me a happy day;
and if my love is true,
I must no longer hope.
When will you ever reward
my lengthy servitude?"

Plate Ia. Title page of volume 2 of the manuscript collection of Steffani's chamber duets (including revised versions), which was begun by the composer in 1702–3 and completed by 1710. London, British Library, RM 23. k. 14; actual size: 22.75 x 17.25 cm.

Plate Ib. Opening of *Pria ch'io faccia altrui palese* in the hand of the composer. London, British Library, RM 23. k. 14, fol. 1 (p. 1).

Plate IIa. Title page of the presentation manuscript set of
chamber duets apparently intended for Sophie Charlotte, Queen of Prussia.
London, British Library, RM 23. k. 7; actual size: 32 x 27 cm.

Plate IIb. Opening of *Ravvediti, mio core* in an unidentified
copyist's hand, with examples of the "wavy line" ornament (m. 6).
London, British Library, RM 23. k. 7, fol. 49 (p. 97).

TWELVE
CHAMBER DUETS

Pria ch'io faccia altrui palese

[II] **Seconda [strofa]**

8

che __ de- si- o, quel __ che de- si - o: Ba- sta ben _____

-si- o, quel che __ de- si- o, quel __ che de- si- o:

__ che lo sap- pia, ba- sta ben _____ che lo sap- pia A-

Ba- sta ben _____ che lo sap- pia A- mo-

-mo- re, A- mo- re ed i- o, A- mo- re ed

- re, A- mo- re, A- mo- re ed i- o, A-

i- o, A- mo- re ed i- o. Ba- sta ben _____

-mo- re ed i- o, A- mo- re ed i- o, _____ A-

Quanto care al cor voi siete

mai _____ non vi scior- rò, Che se mai non vi rom- pe- te Io già

rò, già mai _____ non __ vi scior- rò, Che se mai non vi rom- pe- te Io già mai _____

mai __ non vi scior- rò   io già mai non vi scior-rò, già mai ___ non_vi scior- rò. Quan-to ca-re al

_non vi scior-rò,   io già mai non vi scior- rò,   già mai _____ non vi scior- rò.

D.S. al Fine

[II]

A- do- ra- ti,   a- do- ra-   ti miei tor-men-   -

A- do- ra- ti,   a- do- ra- ti miei tor- men-

- ti,   Sì, strin- ge-   -   -   te-mi,

- ti,   Sì, strin- ge-   -

[III]

16

17

Ribellatevi, o pensieri

D.S. al Fine

24

[II] [L'istesso tempo]

[Soprano I, II]

[Sop. I]

1. Se per- dei, se per- dei per in- fi- da _ bel- lez- za, ___ Stol- to _ a-
-nir- mi, di scher- nir- mi hai fi- ni- to, _ Cu- pi- do, ___ Fal- so ___

[2nd time]

- man- te, ___ Se per- dei, se per- dei per in- fi- da _ bel- lez- za, ___
nu- me, ___ Di scher- nir- mi, di scher- nir- mi hai fi- ni- to, _ Cu- pi- do, ___

Stol- to _ a- man- te, ___ la mia li- ber- tà, ___
Fal- so ___ nu- me, _ bam- bi- no cru- del, ___

la mia li- ber- tà,
bam- bi- no cru- del;

[Repeat "Ribellatevi, o pensieri"]

Su, ferisci, alato arciero

28

32

stral, _____ il tuo stral _____

_____ non fa mo- rir, non fa mo-

_ non fa mo- rir, non fa mo- rir, non fa mo- rir, non fa mo- rir.

- rir, non fa mo- rir, non fa mo- rir, non fa, non fa mo- rir.

[II] [Tempo di gavotta]

[Soprano I] 1. Che tor- men- to può dar un guar- do __ Che s'in- con- tra,
[Soprano II] 2. Qual mar- ti- re può dar quel se- no __ In cui fis- so,

Che tor- men- to può dar un guar- do __ Che s'in- con- tra __ con pia- cer, _____
Qual mar- ti- re può dar quel se- no __ In cui fis- so __ sta'l de- sir, _____

*The editor suggests ♩ ♪ throughout.

che s'in- con- tra con_ pia- cer?
in cui fis- so sta'l_ de- sir?

Fe- ra_ pur, fe- ra_ pur il nu- me- cie- co, Se'l suo_ dar- do Por- ta_
Po- ca_ nu- be, po- ca_ nu- be è quel tor- men- to, Ch'il se- re- no D'un con-

- se- co La spe- ran- za_ di go- der, _____
-ten- to In bre- v'o- ra_ fa spa- rir, _____

[Se'l suo_ dar- do_ Por- ta_ se- co,]
Ch'il se- re- no_ D'un con- ten- to,

Se'l suo_ dar- do_ Por- ta_ se- co La spe- ran- za_ di go- der.
Ch'il se- re- no_ D'un con- ten- to_ In bre- v'o- ra_ fa spa- rir.

*The editor suggests

[Repeat "Su, ferisci"]

E perché non m'uccidete

[Poet: Brigida Bianchi]

42

[D.C. al Fine]

E così mi compatite?

[Poet: Brigida Bianchi]

[Soprano]

1. E co- sì mi com- pa- ti- te? Che mi
2. E co- sì mi con- so- la- te? Per con-

[Tenor]

1. E co- sì mi com- pa- ti- te,
2. E co- sì mi con- so- la- te,

gio- va, o lu- ci in- gra- te, ___ Di ser- vir _____
-for- to ___ del mio duo- lo ___ Io vi chie-

e co- sì mi com- pa- ti- te,
e co- sì mi con- so- la- te,

se mi sprez- za- te, Di ___ lan- guir se mi ___ scher- ni-
-do un guar- do so- lo E ___ voi cru- de me'l ___ ne- ga-

e co-
e co-

48

-te. E co-sì mi com-pa- ti- te, e co- sì_____ mi____

-te, e co- sì mi com-pa- ti- te, e co- sì_____

_____ com- pa- ti- - te, mi____ com- pa- ti- te?

____ mi_____ com- pa- ti- te, mi_____ com- pa- ti- te?

Da Capo [seconda strofa] al Segno, poi segue

Io di pian- to a- sper- go il ci- glio, Ad- di- tan- do-vi il

mio ar- dor,_____ ad- di- tan- do____ il mio ar- dor,

Saldi marmi, che coprite

-ri- re, o___ pur mo- ri- re,_____ o___ pur mo- ri-

_ o___ pur mo- ri- re,_____ o___ pur mo-

- re, o pur, o pur mo- ri- re,___ o___ pur mo- ri- re?"

-ri- re, o pur, o pur mo- ri- re, o___ pur mo- ri- re?"

[II] Solo [recitativo]

[Soprano I or II]

Co- sì Fil- le di- ce- a, Del suo per- du- to be- ne Ri- vol- ta un

gior- no al- le bel- lez- ze e- stin- te. Vis- s'el- la di Fi- le- no Lun- ga sta-

-gio- ne   in for-tu- na- ti a-   mo- ri;   Ma già   le bion-de_a-ri- ste

Quat-tro vol- te di- vi- se_a-vea dal suo- lo   Del cur- vo mie- ti- tor   la fal- ce a-dun-ca   Da

ch'ei, ce-den-do_a mor- te,   Tra so- li- ta- rii ar-dor   la- sciol- la   in vi- ta;

[a tempo]

Non van-târ mai, tra tan- to,   Lac- ci_un crin,   ri- si_un

[recitativo]

lab- bro, O stra-   - li un ci- glio,   on-de_il suo cor fe- de- le

O pia- ga- to, o in- va- ghi- to, o av- vin- to fos- se. Mo-

-strol- le al fi- ne il ca- so Ne' be- gl'oc- chi di Tir- si Del- l'a- ma- to Fi- len mil- le sem-

-bian- ze; On- de, fat- ta in- ca- pa- ce Di re- si- ster al bel ch'a- mò u- na vol- ta,

Ri- so- lu- ta d'a- ma- re an- co- ra un dì, Par- lan- do a' pen- sier suo-

-i, dis- se co- sì, co- sì, dis- se co- sì, par- lan- do a' pen- sier suo- i, par-

-lan-do_a' pen-sier suo- i, dis- - se co- sì, co- sì, dis- se co- sì, co- sì, co- sì, dis- se co- sì:

[attacca]

[III]

"In- co- stan- - za, e che pre-ten- di, e che, e che pre-ten-

"In- co- stan-

- di, in- co- stan- - za, e che pre- ten- di, e che, e

- za, in- co- stan- - za, e che pre-ten- di, e che, e che, e

che pre- ten- di, in- co- stan- za, e che pre-ten- di, e che,

che pre-ten- di, e che, in co- stan- - za, e

60

Ravvediti, mio core

rav- ve- di-ti, rav- ve- di-ti, mio co- re, rav- ve- di-

co- re, rav- ve- di- ti, mio co- re, rav- ve- di- ti, rav-

-ti, rav- ve- di- ti, rav- ve- di- ti, mio co- re.

-ve- di- ti, mio co- re.

[II]

Non han for- za i miei la- men- ti D'im-pe- trar pie- to- sa,

Non han

pie- to- sa a- i- ta, pie- to- sa a- i- ta; Non han for- za i

for- za i miei la- men- ti D'im-pe- trar pie- to- sa, pie- to-

miei la- men-ti D'im-pe- trar pie to- sa, pie to- sa a-
-sa a- i-ta, pie to-sa a- i- ta, d'im-pe- trar pie to-
-i- ta, pie to-sa a- i- ta; Non han for- za i miei la-
-sa a- i- ta; Non han for- za i miei la- men- ti, non han
-men- ti D'im- pe-trar pie to- sa, pie to- sa a-
for- za i miei la- men- ti D'im-pe-trar pie to- sa a- i- ta, pie-
-i-ta, pie to-sa a i- ta; È ca- gion de' miei tor- men-
-to- sa a- i- ta;

[III] **Seconda parte**

il tuo bar- - ba-ro ri-

-ba-ro ri-go- re, il tuo bar- -ba-ro ri-

-go- re, Che pre- ten- di dal mio co- re, A- do- ra- ta, a- do- ra-

-go- re, Che pre- ten- di dal mio co- re,

- ta mia ti-ran- na? Che pre- ten- di dal mio co- re,

che pre- ten- di dal mio co- re, A- do- ra- ta, a- do-

A- do- ra- ta, a- do- ra- - ta mia ti-ran-

-ra- ta, a- do- ra- - ta mia ti-ran- na, a- do-

Vorrei dire un non so che

45

Ma la lin- gua m'an- no- da A-mor, Né__ co- no-scer, né__ co- no-scer so__ per- ché.

-no-da A-mor, Né__ co- no-scer so__ per- ché, né__ co- scer so per- ché.

[II] Solo [recitativo]

[Soprano]

U- di- ste mai più stra-no ca- so, o bel- la? So che voi so- la

sie- te Ca-gion del mio mar- ti- re, E non ve lo so di- re. Cie-co Amor si ser-vì

de' vo- stri lu- mi Per far ch'io mi con-su- mi,__ E la

[a tempo]

sua cru-del- tà tan-to s'e-sten- de Che quan- do io son con

voi mu- - to, mu- - to mi

ren- de, che quan- do io son con voi

mu- - to, mu- - to mi ren- - de.

[III] **Solo [recitativo]**

[Tenor]

Quan- do lon- tan da vo- i Pas-so mi- se- re l'o- re, M'e- sce per

gl'oc-chi, m'e- sce per gl'oc-chi il fo- co, ch'ho nel co- re

Stra-va-gan- ze d'a- mo- re. Quan-d'io vi son vi- ci- no, Lan-gui- sco, pe- no,

[a tempo]

mo- ro; Ma non vi sa-prei dir, ma non vi sa-prei

dir, bel- la, v'a- do- ro, bel-

- la, v'a- do- ro, ma non vi sa-prei dir, bel- la, v'a-

-do- ro, bel- -

Occhi belli, non più

90

-bon- do i miei ne- mi- ci a- do- ro. ___

-te, Per- ch'io tra-fit- to mo-

Deh, non più sa- et- ta- te, non

-ro E___ mo- ri- bon- do,

più sa- et- ta- te, Per-

e___ mo- ri- bon- do i miei ne- mi- ci a- do- ro. ___

-ch'io tra-fit- to mo- ro E___ mo- ri-

Deh, non più sa- et- ta-

[II] Solo

[Soprano]

Ren- di- ti, ren- di- ti‿o- mai, mio co- re, ren- di- ti, ren- di- ti‿o-

-mai, mio co- re, E la- scia la bat- ta-

- - - glia, or che non puo- i Re- si- ster con- tro do- i, E

la- scia la bat- ta- - glia, e la- scia la bat- ta-

-to, un se- mi- mor- to, un_

_ se- mi- mor- to, con- tro dop- pio_ ne- mi- co un_____

_ se- mi- mor- - - to,

un se- mi- mor- - to, un_ se- mi- mor- to.

[III] Solo

[Tenor]

Per- ché, lu- mi bu- giar- di, Of- frir- mi

[IV]

Begl'occhi, oh Dio, non più

106

[III] **Solo [recitativo]**

[Soprano]

le, ti fa, ti___ fa cru- de- le.

Se la tua ge- lo- si- a È par- te del tuo a-

-mor, o bel- la Clo- ri, Che fia dun- que, che

fi- a? Quan-do de'miei do- lo- ri Do- vrò spe- ra- re il fin?

[a tempo]

Men-tre con-vie-ne Che, per- ché trop- po m'a- mi, io

110

vi- va in pe - ne, io vi- va in pe-

-ne, che, per- ché trop- po m'a- mi,

io vi- - va in pe- - ne, io vi- va in_ pe- ne.

[IV]

Clo- ri mi- a, Clo- ri mi- a, deh, fer- ma al- quan-

Clo- ri mi- a, Clo- ri

112

*The editor suggests ♩♪ throughout

* The editor suggests ♩ ♪ throughout

Aure, voi che volate

[a tempo]

Ch'o-da da me'l mio duol, voi glie'l nar- ra- te, Zef- fi- ret- ti cor-

-te- si, zef- fi- ret- ti cor- te- si, au-

- ret- -

- te gra- te, zef- fi- ret- ti cor-

-te- si, au- ret- -

122

[attacca]

123

124

D.S. al Fine